P9-ELD-473

The Cam Jansen Series

Cam Jansen and the Mystery of the Stolen Diamonds
Cam Jansen and the Mystery of the U.F.O.
Cam Jansen and the Mystery of the Dinosaur Bones
Cam Jansen and the Mystery of the Television Dog
Cam Jansen and the Mystery of the Gold Coins
Cam Jansen and the Mystery of the Babe Ruth Baseball
Cam Jansen and the Mystery of the Circus Clown
Cam Jansen and the Mystery of the Monster Movie
Cam Jansen and the Mystery of the Carnival Prize
Cam Jansen and the Mystery at the Monkey House
Cam Jansen and the Mystery of the Stolen Corn Popper
Cam Jansen and the Mystery of Flight 54
Cam Jansen and the Mystery at the Haunted House
Cam Jansen and the Chocolate Fudge Mystery
Cam Jansen and the Triceratops Pops Mystery
Cam Jansen and the Ghostly Mystery
Cam Jansen and the Scary Snake Mystery
Cam Jansen and the Catnapping Mystery
Cam Jansen and the Barking Treasure Mystery
Cam Jansen and the Birthday Mystery
Cam Jansen and the School Play Mystery
Cam Jansen and the First Day of School Mystery
Cam Jansen and the Tennis Trophy Mystery
Cam Jansen and the Snowy Day Mystery
Cam Jansen and the Valentine Baby Mystery—25th Anniversary Special
Cam Jansen and the Secret Service Mystery
Cam Jansen and the Summer Camp Mysteries—A Super Special
Cam Jansen and the Mystery Writer Mystery
Cam Jansen and the Green School Mystery
Cam Jansen and the Sports Day Mysteries—A Super Special
Cam Jansen and the Basketball Mystery
Cam Jansen and the Wedding Cake Mystery
Cam Jansen and the Graduation Day Mystery

DON'T FORGET ABOUT THE YOUNG CAM JANSEN
SERIES FOR YOUNGER READERS!

CamJansen

and the
Millionaire
Mystery

David A. Adler

illustrated by
Joy Allen

VIKING
An Imprint of Penguin Group (USA) Inc.

VIKING
Published by the Penguin Group
Penguin Young Readers Group, 345 Hudson Street, New York, New York 10014, U.S.A.
Penguin Group (Canada), 90 Eglinton Avenue East, Suite 700, Toronto, Ontario,
Canada M4P 2Y3 (a division of Pearson Penguin Canada Inc.)
Penguin Books Ltd, 80 Strand, London WC2R 0RL, England
Penguin Ireland, 25 St Stephen's Green, Dublin 2,
Ireland (a division of Penguin Books Ltd)
Penguin Group (Australia), 250 Camberwell Road, Camberwell, Victoria 3124,
Australia (a division of Pearson Australia Group Pty Ltd)
Penguin Books India Pvt Ltd, 11 Community Centre, Panchsheel Park,
New Delhi – 110 017, India
Penguin Group (NZ), 67 Apollo Drive, Rosedale, Auckland 0632,
New Zealand (a division of Pearson New Zealand Ltd.)
Penguin Books (South Africa) (Pty) Ltd, 24 Sturdee Avenue, Rosebank, Johannesburg
2196, South Africa

Penguin Books Ltd, Registered Offices: 80 Strand, London WC2R 0RL, England

First published in the United States of America by Viking,
a division of Penguin Young Readers Group, 2012

1   3   5   7   9   10   8   6   4   2

Text copyright © David Adler, 2012
Illustrations copyright © Penguin Young Readers Group, 2012
All rights reserved

LIBRARY OF CONGRESS CATALOGING-IN-PUBLICATION DATA
Adler, David A.
Cam Jansen and the millionaire mystery / by David A. Adler.
p. cm.—(Cam Jansen ; [32])
Summary: Using her excellent memory, Cam Jansen, aided by her friend
Eric, investigates the disappearance of Mrs. Scott's valuable pearl
necklace during a charity brunch.
ISBN 978-0-670-01258-9 (hardcover)
[1. Lost and found possessions—Fiction. 2. Stealing—Fiction.
3. Memory—Fiction. 4. Mystery and detective stories.] I. Title.
PZ7.A2615Caaej 2011   [Fic]—dc23   2011039464

Printed in China
Set in ITC New Baskerville Std

For my Young Aunt Judy
—D.A.A.

Dedicated to the Cameron Park
Fire Department!
Awesome you are.
—J.A.

Cam Jansen

and the
Millionaire
Mystery

Chapter One

"May I take your coats?" the man at the front door asked.

"Will he give them back?" Eric Shelton whispered to his mother.

"Yes. When we're ready to leave, he'll give them back."

The man was wearing a fancy black suit and small black bow tie.

Eric and his mother gave the man their coats. So did Cam Jansen and her mother. They were at the apartment of Ellen and Aaron Scott for a charity brunch. The apartment was on the top two floors of one of the tallest buildings in the city.

1

"Thank you for coming," a woman in a fireman's uniform told people as they entered the apartment. She smiled at Cam and Eric. She gave them each a red plastic fire hat.

The brunch was to raise money for a new firehouse.

Cam and Eric put on the hats. Then they all walked into a large dining room. On the table were trays of food.

"Look at all the fish and salads," Mrs. Shelton said.

"Look at all the cake and cookies," Eric said.

A waiter gave them each a plate.

"Fish and salad first," Mrs. Jansen told Cam and Eric. "Cake and cookies later."

Cam and Eric put some food on their plates. While they were eating, an old woman in a long gray dress stood by the entrance to the room. She tapped on a large glass.

Ting! Ting! Ting!

People in the room stopped eating and talking.

"I'm Ellen Scott," the woman announced. "Welcome to my home. Later, I hope you'll come upstairs. There are more desserts there. Music will be played, and from our large windows, you'll see beautiful views of—"

Ellen Scott stopped talking. She was staring at Cam.

"Are you that girl with the great memory?" she asked.

"Yes," Cam's mother said. "This is my daughter, Cam Jansen, and she does have a great memory. It's as if she has a camera in her head and pictures of everything she's ever seen."

Ellen Scott stood next to Cam. She tapped on her glass again.

Ting! Ting! Ting!

"We have a celebrity here! Surely you've all read in the local newspapers about Cam Jansen? She's the girl who uses her amazing photographic memory to solve mysteries. She's even helped catch criminals."

Ellen Scott smiled at Cam and applauded. Others in the room applauded, too.

"Watch this," Eric said loudly. Everyone looked at Eric.

He turned to Cam and said, "Look at me and say, *'Click!'* Then close your eyes."

Cam looked at Eric.

"No! No!" Ellen Scott said. "Look at me."

Cam Jansen looked at Ellen Scott. She said, *"Click!"* and closed her eyes.

Eric told the people in the room, "Cam says, *'Click!'* when she wants to remember something. It's the sound her mental camera makes."

"Turn around," Eric whispered, "so no one will think you're peeking."

Cam turned around. She was no longer facing Ellen Scott.

Mrs. Scott asked Cam, "What color dress am I wearing?"

"Gray. It has seven large buttons in front. You're wearing a pearl necklace, four bracelets on your right wrist, and a gold watch on your left wrist."

Then Cam whispered, "Your third button is open."

Ellen Scott looked down at her dress. She closed the third button.

When Cam was born, her parents named her Jennifer. But when people found out about her great memory, they started calling her "The Camera." Soon, "The Camera" became just "Cam."

"You're truly amazing," Mrs. Scott said.

"Thank you for your performance, Miss Jansen," an elderly man said.

Then he spoke to the many other people in the room.

"I'm Aaron Scott. We are so grateful you are all here to help us build a new firehouse. I hope you'll all join us upstairs to see a beautiful view of our fine city. You may take the stairs or go by elevator."

Cam turned and opened her eyes.

"I'm taking the elevator," Mrs. Scott told Cam. "Please come with me. I want to ask you all about the mysteries you've solved."

Chapter Two

Cam and her mother followed Mrs. Scott to the elevator. Eric and his mother followed Mr. Scott to the stairs.

"When did you first know you had a great memory?" Mrs. Scott asked.

"It was me. I was the first to realize it," Mrs. Jansen said. "When Cam was little I read to her every night. One night I was in a hurry and skipped a page. 'No, Mommy,' Cam said. 'What about the man with the blue shirt, red pants, and sneakers?' She described everything on that page. After that we had lots of fun playing all sorts of memory games. Cam was just two years old, but she always won."

"That's amazing," Mrs. Scott said.

The elevator doors opened. Cam and her mother followed Mrs. Scott onto the elevator.

"Does your great memory help you with your schoolwork?"

"Cam does very well in school," Mrs. Jansen said.

"It's easy for me to remember spelling words," Cam said. "And I always remember what I read."

"Is there room for me?" asked a woman wearing a long green dress and carrying a large open handbag. "I have trouble with stairs."

"Of course there's room," Mrs. Scott told the woman. She waved her hand and told her to come onto the elevator.

"In class I always raise my hand, but my teacher hardly ever calls on me," Cam told Mrs. Scott. "She says, 'I'm sure you remember the work. I want to find out if others in the class remember.'"

An old man with a cane got on the elevator.

Another old man and his wife got on. They were friends of Mrs. Scott.

"This is such a nice party," the man said.

A man wearing a dark blue jacket and holding a paper coffee cup came on.

A woman wearing a tight flowered dress was about to get on. She was holding a plate with a gooey piece of cake.

"Please eat that first," the old man with the cane said. "I don't want that messy cake to get on my clothes."

The woman quickly ate the cake. She licked the gooey icing off her fingers. Then she gave the plate to a waiter and got on the elevator.

A young man in a fireman's uniform got on.

"That's it," Mrs. Scott said. "There's no more room."

Mrs. Scott was standing by a set of buttons. She pushed a button and the elevator doors closed.

"We're going up," Mrs. Scott said.

Cam and her mother were pressed against the wall of the elevator. Cam took a deep breath and held it. Then the doors opened and people got out. Cam exhaled.

"The big windows are to your right," Mrs. Scott announced.

"Let's go see," Mrs. Jansen said. "We parked our car right in front. I bet from up here it looks like a little toy."

Cam turned to Mrs. Scott.

"Thanks for the ride," Cam said.

Cam stopped.

"Oh," she said. "I think something is missing."

Cam closed her eyes. She said, *"Click!"*

Cam quickly opened her eyes. "Mrs. Scott," she said, "your pearl necklace is gone!"

Chapter Three

Mrs. Scott reached up. She felt her neck. Then she hurried to look in the mirror by the elevator.

"This is terrible," she said. "Aaron bought the necklace for my birthday."

She pressed the button by the elevator. The doors opened. She looked on the floor.

"The clasp must have opened. It must have fallen to the floor. I hope no one stepped on it."

Cam, Mrs. Jansen, and Mrs. Scott bent down and checked the thick carpet near the elevator.

Eric and his mother were just coming up the stairs.

"Did you lose something?" Eric asked.

Cam told him about the necklace.

"Someone must have stolen it," Eric said. "This is another mystery. We have to find the necklace and the thief."

Mrs. Scott looked at the many people in her apartment.

"Aaron, Aaron," she called.

Mr. Scott hurried to her.

"Are you tired? Is this party too much?"

"No, it's not that," Mrs. Scott said, shaking her head.

She told her husband about the necklace.

Mr. Scott gasped.

"It was stolen," Eric told him.

"The boy is right," Mr. Scott said. "That necklace is very valuable. It has a double clasp. I saw you lock it this morning. It couldn't have just fallen off. I'm calling security."

Mr. Scott hurried away.

"Oh, I hope they find it," Mrs. Scott said. "We have very good security here. They watch everyone who enters and leaves this building."

"I noticed that," Mrs. Jansen said. "When we arrived, the woman at the door asked us our names. She had a list of who was coming to the party. She even made me show her my driver's license."

Mr. Scott was back.

"That nice guard Amy is coming right up," he said. "I also called the police. They told me not to let anyone leave the apartment. I put someone at each door."

"I bet the thief will try to leave," Mrs. Shelton said.

"Did you feel anyone pulling at your necklace?" Mr. Scott asked.

His wife shook her head.

"The elevator was crowded. People were pressed against me, but I would have noticed if someone pulled the necklace."

There was a chair by the elevator. Mr. Scott sat down and said, "We have more than one hundred guests. Any one of them might be the thief."

"No," Cam told him. "It could only be

someone who was in the elevator with us."

Mr. Scott asked his wife, "Do you remember who was on the elevator?"

"There were Jane and Joe Levy. Cam Jansen and her mother were with me."

Mrs. Scott thought for a moment.

"There were other people on the elevator," she said. "I just don't remember who."

Cam closed her eyes. She said, *"Click!"* Then, with her eyes still closed she said, "I remember them. I remember them all."

"I'm here," a woman in green uniform said.

Cam opened her eyes.

"Hi, Amy," Mr. Scott said. "Did anyone leave my apartment in the last ten minutes?"

"No one left the building," Amy said.

She looked around the apartment. "It's someone here, and I'll check them all. I'll find the thief."

"Whoever took the necklace was on the elevator with us," Cam told Amy. "There were ten of us."

"Ten? You must have been squeezed in there."

"We were," Mrs. Scott said. "But it's a short ride."

"The police are here," Amy said. "I'll talk to them. I'll tell them what happened."

"Tell them it's an expensive necklace," Mr. Scott said. "Very expensive."

Two police officers had come into the room. Amy spoke with them. Then the two officers walked over to Mrs. Scott.

"This is Cam Jansen," Mrs. Scott said. "She knows who was on the elevator with me."

Cam closed her eyes and said, *"Click!"* Then, with her eyes still closed she described the people on the elevator.

"There was Mrs. Scott. I was there with my mother."

"That's me," Mrs. Jansen said.

"There was a woman in a long green dress,

a man wearing a fireman's uniform, and an old man with a cane. There were two people, a man and a woman. They're Mrs. Scott's friends."

"Jane and Joe Levy," Mrs. Scott said. "But they didn't take my necklace."

One of the officers wrote Cam's descriptions in his police notepad.

"There was a man wearing a blue jacket and tie, and there was a woman who wanted

to get on with some sticky cake, but she didn't.
First she finished the cake."

Cam opened her eyes.

"That's it," Cam said. "That's everyone."

"We have to check them all," one of the
officers said. He looked right at Cam and
Mrs. Jansen. "We even have to check you."

Chapter Four

"Is there an empty room we can use?" one of the officers asked the Scotts. "We need a place to bring all the suspects."

"You can use the library."

Across from the elevator were two large doors. Mrs. Scott opened them.

The walls of the room were lined with bookcases. One bookcase had glass doors. There were several large chairs in the room.

"Please come in here," one of the officers told Cam and Mrs. Jansen.

Cam and her mother went into the library. Eric and Mrs. Shelton went in, too.

"I'm Officer Jack Kaplan. I need you to empty your pockets."

Mrs. Jansen whispered to Cam, "We're suspects. He thinks we might have taken the necklace."

Cam took a pen and a small notepad from her pockets.

"That's all I have," Cam said.

She pulled out the inside of her pockets and showed Officer Kaplan that they were empty.

Mrs. Jansen emptied her pockets. She took paperclips, cough drops, coins, keys, coupons, a shopping list, and small bits of thread from her pockets. She opened her handbag and Officer Kaplan looked through it.

The other officer was standing by the door to the library. "Come with me," she told Mrs. Scott. "We have to find the other people who were on the elevator."

"Let's take Cam with us," Mrs. Scott told the officer. "I don't remember everyone who was with us, but she does."

"Let's go," the officer told Cam.

They walked toward the many large windows overlooking the city.

"I'm Officer Sally Phillips. Whoever took the necklace must have it in his or her pocket or handbag, so we'll have to check them all."

The party guests had gathered by the windows.

"That's where I work," a woman said as she looked out over the city.

Cam pointed to a woman in a tight flowered dress. "She was on the elevator," Cam whispered. "She was holding a plate of cake."

"She's eating more of that cake now," Mrs. Scott whispered. "She must really like it."

Officer Phillips spoke with the woman. Then they walked together to the library.

"There are Jane and Joe Levy," Cam said.

Mrs. Scott spoke to her friends. She told them to go to the library.

Officer Phillips was back. "We still have a few more people to find," she said to Cam and Mrs. Scott.

"Four more," Cam said.

Cam walked slowly past the many people standing by the windows.

"I can see my house," someone said, and pointed.

"I can see my store," someone else said.

"Officer Phillips," Cam whispered. "That

woman in the green dress was on the elevator. She got on right after we did. And that man with the cane was with us."

Officer Phillips spoke to both of them. She walked with them to the library.

"Wasn't that man in the uniform also on the elevator?" Mrs. Scott asked.

Cam looked at the man. She closed her eyes and said, *"Click!"*

"Yes," Cam said.

Mrs. Scott asked the man to follow her to the library.

One more, Cam thought. There was one more person on the elevator.

Cam said, *"Click!"* again. She looked at the pictures she had in her head of the people on the elevator.

Officer Phillips and Mrs. Scott had returned from the library.

"Is that it?" Officer Phillips asked.

Cam opened her eyes.

"There's one more," Cam said. "He was wearing a dark blue jacket and tie. I looked at everyone standing by the windows and I didn't find him."

"Are there any other rooms up here?"

"There are two bedrooms," Mrs. Scott told Officer Phillips, "but the doors to those rooms are closed."

"Let's check."

Mrs. Scott led them to two doors, one on either side of a wide hallway. Officer Sally Phillips checked both doors. They were locked.

"Maybe he went downstairs," Mrs. Scott said. "Maybe he wanted more fish and salad, and that's served only downstairs."

Cam, Mrs. Scott, and Officer Phillips walked toward the elevator. Just then a door in the hall was opened. It was the door to the bathroom. A man wearing a dark blue jacket walked out.

"That's him," Cam told Officer Phillips. "He was on the elevator with us."

Chapter Five

"Please come with me," Officer Phillips told the man in the blue jacket.

"What did I do?"

"I didn't say you did anything. I just asked you to come along."

They all went to the library.

Officer Kaplan was there with the six other people who were on the elevator with Cam, her mother, and Mrs. Scott. Eric and Mrs. Shelton were there, too.

Officer Kaplan wrote the man's name next to the description he had in his note-pad. Then he asked the man to empty his pockets.

"But I didn't do anything."

The man took a wallet from his back pants pocket. He took a few coins from one of his front pockets. Then he pulled the inside of each pocket out so the officers could see they were empty.

"Is that everyone?" Officer Kaplan asked Mrs. Scott.

Mrs. Scott looked at Cam.

"There were ten of us on the elevator," Cam said, "and we're all here."

"What are you looking for?" Jane Levy asked. She was Mrs. Scott's friend. "Maybe we saw it."

"We're looking for a valuable pearl necklace," Officer Kaplan said. "Mrs. Scott was wearing it when she got on the elevator. When she got off, it was gone."

Officer Phillips sat in one of the big library chairs. She looked at the many people in the room.

"Can I go now?" the woman in the green dress asked. "I'm not a thief. You know I don't have the necklace. By now my husband must be looking for me."

"Yes," the old man with the cane said. "I'm also not a thief. I'm an accountant, and I came with my daughter."

"That's it!" Officer Phillips said.

She got out of her chair. She looked at the woman in the green dress and said, "You came with your husband." She looked at the old man. "You came with your daughter. Each of you came with someone. One of you

took the necklace, but you no longer have it. You must have given it to your partner."

Mrs. Scott said, "The doorman has a list of everyone at the brunch. The names are in groups. They're listed the way they made the reservations."

"We were listed with the Sheltons," Mrs. Jansen said.

"Please empty your pockets," Officer Phillips told the Sheltons.

Mrs. Shelton and Eric emptied their pockets. Of course, they didn't have the necklace.

"This is not right," the man wearing the blue jacket said. "I came to help support the new firehouse and now I'm being treated like a common criminal."

"Please be patient, sir. I'll bring in the people listed with all of you," Officer Phillips said. "I'm sure we'll find the necklace, and then you can all go."

Officer Phillips left the library.

Officer Kaplan stood by the door.

Eric whispered to Cam, "Do you think they'll find the thief?"

"Yes," Cam whispered. "The thief had to be someone on the elevator. No one here

has the necklace. That means he or she must have given it to someone."

Mrs. Shelton and a few of the other people in the room looked at the many books in the library.

"May I take a book out?" Mrs. Shelton asked.

"Oh, yes," Mrs. Scott said. "You may even borrow some, just not the ones in the book-case with the glass doors. Those are valuable first editions."

Eric whispered to Cam, "Everything in this apartment is valuable. I bet that's why the thief came here. The thief didn't come to help the firehouse. He or she came to steal something."

Officer Phillips opened the door of the library. A tall man in a dark brown suit came in. He hurried to the woman in the green dress.

"What's this all about?" he asked.

"Something was stolen."

"Please empty your pockets," Officer Kaplan said.

"But I didn't take anything."

"Just do it," his wife told him.

The man took out a wallet, a cell phone, keys, coins, a pen, and business cards.

Officer Phillips opened the door again. A young woman, the daughter of the old man with the cane, came in. She emptied her pockets and handbag. She didn't have the necklace.

"That's everyone," Officer Phillips said. "The others came alone."

"What will you do now?" Mrs. Scott asked. "How will you find my necklace?"

"I don't know," Officer Phillips said, shaking her head. "I don't know."

"What are you thinking?" Eric whispered to Cam.

"I'm thinking the thief is one of the people in this room and is very clever. Somehow the thief either hid the necklace or got it out of the apartment."

Chapter Six

"Can I go now?" the woman in the green dress asked.

"I'm not asking. I'm just going," the man in the blue jacket said.

He started toward the door.

Officer Kaplan opened his notepad. He read his notes. Then he looked at the many people in the library.

"We really can't keep them any longer," Officer Kaplan told his partner.

Officer Phillips opened the door and told the people in the library, "Thank you for your cooperation. You may go now."

"Is that it?" Eric asked Cam. "They're just going to let the thief keep the necklace?"

Cam watched as people left the library.

"We know the thief doesn't have the necklace right now," Cam whispered. "But whoever stole the necklace must know where it is. When the thief thinks no one is looking, he or she will go get it."

Cam, Eric, Mrs. Jansen, and Mrs. Shelton left the library.

"I'm going downstairs for some more salad," Eric's mother said.

"I'll go with you," Mrs. Jansen said.

"We'll be right back," they told Cam and Eric.

Cam and Eric waited in the hall by the library. They watched their mothers walk to the spiral staircase.

"I wonder what the people from the elevator are doing now," Cam said.

"There's that woman in the flowered dress," Eric said. "She's getting another piece of cake."

Cam looked at her. Then she looked at all the people standing by the large windows.

Cam pointed to Jane and Joe Levy. They were talking with Ellen and Aaron Scott. She pointed to the old man with the cane. He was sitting on a chair by one of the large windows. His daughter was with him. The old man's cane was leaning against the arm of the chair.

"Some canes are hollow," Eric said. "I saw a spy movie, and a secret map was hidden in a cane."

Cam looked at the old man.

"I watched him when he left the library," Eric said. "He walks fine. I don't even think he needs a cane."

"You think the necklace is inside his cane?" Eric nodded.

"Then why is he still here?" Cam asked. "Why doesn't he leave with his cane before the police find out what he did?"

Mrs. Jansen and Mrs. Shelton came up the stairs. Mrs. Shelton had two plates of salad.

"Look what I brought for you," Mrs. Shelton said. She gave Eric a plate and a fork. "It's spinach salad. It's delicious."

Eric tasted the salad.

"It's not delicious," he told his mother.

"It's good for you," Mrs. Shelton said. "Spinach has lots of vitamins and calcium. It has iron and copper."

"Iron and copper!" Eric said. "Those are metals. I'm not eating metal."

"They're also names of nutrients. They're good for you."

Eric nibbled his salad.

The old man held onto the arms of his chair and got up. He started toward the elevator. His daughter went with him.

"Look," Eric whispered. "He forgot his cane."

Eric gave his mother his salad. He went and took the cane from the chair. Cam went with him. As Eric walked toward the elevator he tried to twist off the top of the cane. He couldn't. He shook the cane.

"There's nothing inside," he whispered to Cam.

The elevator doors started to close. Cam pushed the button by the side of the elevator. The doors opened. Eric gave the old man his cane.

"Thank you," he said. "I keep forgetting that."

Cam and Eric returned to their mothers. Eric's mother gave him his salad. Eric nibbled on a spinach leaf.

"Hey," Cam said. "Look over there."

She pointed to the man in the dark blue jacket.

"He's standing by the windows but he's looking this way. He's looking toward the doors to the library."

Eric nibbled on another piece of spinach.

"Why isn't he looking at the view?" Cam asked.

Cam looked at the man. Then she closed her eyes and said, *"Click!"*

"That's it!" Cam said, opening her eyes. "Some people in the elevator were carrying things."

"The old man had a cane," Eric said. "And some of the women had handbags."

"But they still had those things when they were in the library," Cam said. "The police checked them. But that man had something

in the elevator that he didn't have in the library."

"He did?"

"He had a coffee cup."

"It was a paper cup," Eric said. "He probably finished his coffee and threw the cup away."

"Did he?" Cam asked. "Or did he hide the necklace in the cup and then hide the cup? Is he looking this way to see if anyone is watching? Is he just waiting to get the necklace and leave the party?"

Chapter Seven

"Follow his eyes," Eric whispered. "I think he's looking at the small table near the elevator. Do you see those two paper cups on the table? I bet one of them is his."

Cam looked at the cups.

"The necklace must be in one of the cups," Eric said. "He got off the elevator and quickly got rid of the cup. He put it on that table. Now he's just watching to make sure no one takes it. Then, when no one is looking, he'll take the cup and necklace and leave the party."

"Let's find out," Cam whispered. "Let's

each take one of those cups and see what he does."

Cam and Eric walked to the table by the elevator. They each took a cup.

"I'm afraid to look," Eric said. "What's he doing?"

"He's just watching us."

Cam and Eric returned to the hall by the library.

"What are you doing with those dirty cups?" Mrs. Shelton asked. "They're covered with germs."

"Mine is empty," Cam said.

"Mine has a napkin in it," Eric said. "I bet Mrs. Scott's necklace is under it."

Eric lifted the napkin. He didn't find the necklace.

There was another small table by the doors to the library. Cam and Eric put the empty cups on that table.

"There are empty cups everywhere," Cam said. "The necklace could be in any one of them."

Eric nibbled on another spinach leaf. It was the last one on his plate. He finished it and was about to put his plate on the table.

"I'll take that," a waiter said.

The waiter took Eric's plate and the two cups from the table. Cam and Eric watched as he collected empty plates and cups from the many small tables in the apartment.

"I was wrong," Cam said, and shook her head. "A paper cup wouldn't be a good place to hide a necklace. The waiters collect them and throw them out."

"The police are here," Mrs. Jansen said. "They'll find the necklace. Let's go to those big windows and look at the view. Maybe we can see the harbor and the bridge and your school from here."

As they walked toward the windows, Cam said, "If that man left the necklace in his coffee cup, it's gone. By now a waiter has taken his cup and thrown it and the necklace away."

Mrs. Jansen and Mrs. Shelton stood by the windows and looked out.

"I thought I knew what happened with the necklace," Cam told Eric. "But I was wrong."

"Look at the woman in the flowered dress," Eric whispered. "She's eating another piece of gooey cake."

"That cake must be really good," Eric said. "I'm getting some."

"Me too," Cam said. "I can't solve this mystery, but I can eat cake."

Cam and Eric each took a piece of cake, a fork, and a napkin.

"Mm," Eric said as he tasted the cake. "This is good."

"I can see the harbor from here," Mrs. Jansen said. "The boats look like toys."

"There's your school," Mrs. Shelton said, pointing.

Cam and Eric had finished their cake. There was a trash can in the corner by the windows. Cam and Eric dropped their plates, forks, and napkins in the can.

Mrs. Shelton leaned forward. With her hands she made a pretend pair of binoculars and looked out.

"Eric," she said. "I can see your classroom from here. Your desk is a mess. And you left your science book at school."

"What?"

Eric looked out.

"Hey, you can't see my desk from here."

Mrs. Shelton laughed.

"I was joking," she said. "But I'm sure your desk is a mess, just like at home."

A waiter walked by. He took the cups and plates from the small tables. But he didn't empty the trash can.

"Did you see that?" Cam asked. "The waiters are collecting dirty plates and paper cups but they aren't emptying the trash cans. And I think I know one that surely won't be emp-

tied until after the party. I might know where
to find Mrs. Scott's necklace after all."

Chapter Eight

"I still think the man in the blue jacket took the necklace," Cam said. "He's the only one who took something off the elevator that he didn't have in the library."

Eric turned and looked at the man.

"He's still watching that small table," Eric whispered.

"No, he's watching the door to the bathroom," Cam said.

The door to the bathroom was closed.

"Officer Phillips and I were looking for people who were on the elevator and we found him coming out of there. When he came out, he didn't have the coffee cup."

Cam looked at the man.

"I think he hid the necklace in the cup and he hid the cup in the bathroom. He's waiting for whoever is in there to come out. Then he'll go in and get the necklace."

"I think you're right," Eric said.

Eric and his mother went to find Officers Phillips and Kaplan. Cam moved closer to the bathroom. Mrs. Jansen moved closer, too.

They heard the toilet flush. The door opened and an old woman came out.

The man in the blue jacket hurried to the bathroom. But Cam got in there first. She closed the door and locked it.

"Hey!" The man banged on the door. "I was waiting longer."

"There's another bathroom by the stairs," Mrs. Jansen told him.

"No. I want to use this bathroom. I'll wait until that girl is done." He banged on the door again. "Let me in!"

Cam opened the small cabinet next to the sink. She found tissues, bandages, and aspirin but no necklace. She looked in the cabinet under the sink and found rolls of toilet paper and boxes of tissues. Then she looked at the small wire trash can. It was filled with used tissues.

Germs, Cam thought. *People sneezed in those tissues.*

Cam shook the trash can.

Knock! Knock!

"I'll be right out."

"This is Officer Phillips."

Cam shook the trash can again. A few tissues fell out. Beneath them was a paper coffee cup.

"There it is," Cam said. She reached in for the cup.

Knock! Knock!

"I'm almost done," Cam called out.

There was a paper napkin in the cup. Cam took out the napkin and there it was: Mrs. Scott's pearl necklace.

"I found it! I found it!" Cam called out as she opened the bathroom door. She held up the necklace.

"That's it!" Mrs. Scott said.

Cam told everyone about the man in the blue jacket.

"He was just here," Officer Phillips said.

She took a walkie-talkie from her belt and called Officer Kaplan. She told him to look for the man.

"He's probably on his way out of the building," Mr. Scott said. "I'll call and tell the doorman to stop him."

"I'll go downstairs," Officer Phillips said. "I'll call for extra police."

Mrs. Scott put on the necklace. Her husband closed the clasps.

"Oh, there you are!" a large man in a dark suit called out.

He hurried to the Scotts. A man with a big camera was right behind him.

"Thank you so much for this party and for helping us with the firehouse," he said. "You are great friends of our city."

He kissed Mrs. Scott on her cheek, and the man with the camera took their picture. He grabbed Mr. Scott's hand and shook it. The man with the camera took another picture.

"He's Mayor Kamen," Mrs. Jansen whispered to Cam.

The elevator doors opened. Officer Phillips, Officer Kaplan, and the man in the blue jacket got out. The man's wrists were locked in handcuffs.

"I just wanted you to see that we caught him," Officer Kaplan told the Scotts. "He confessed."

"What? What did he confess?" the mayor asked.

Mrs. Scott told him all about her necklace and how Cam had found it.

"I helped," Eric added.

The mayor stretched out both his arms and declared, "You must both be rewarded."

He grabbed Cam's hand and shook it. Then he shook Eric's hand. The man with the camera took their picture.

"You'll each get copies of that picture. And I'll sign them. You'll have my signature. Isn't that exciting?" the mayor asked.

Cam and Eric didn't answer.

"You'll get hero's medals," the mayor said. "I'll give them to you at city hall. There will be lots of newspaper reporters. This story will be all over the Internet. You'll be famous."

Mayor Kamen stood between Cam and Eric and smiled. The man with the camera took another picture.

The mayor turned to the thief. "Take him to the station house and then to jail," he told Officer Kaplan.

Cam, Eric, and the others watched the thief and the police get on the elevator again. The doors closed.

"Let that be a lesson to everyone," the mayor declared. "Crime does not pay." Then he said, "Let's celebrate."

Everyone followed Mayor Kamen to a table by the windows. He took a huge piece of gooey cake and bit into it. He got icing on his nose, chin, shirt, and tie. The man with him held up his camera.

"No," the mayor said. "Don't take a picture."

He didn't.

But Cam did. She looked at the messy mayor. She blinked her eyes and said, *"Click!"*

A Cam Jansen Memory Game

T ake another look at the picture oppo-
site page 1. Study it. Blink your eyes
and say, *"Click!"* Then turn back here and
answer the questions at the bottom of the
page. Please, first study the picture, *then*
look at the questions.

1. How many people are in the picture?

2. Is Cam smiling?

3. Is anyone wearing a hat?

4. Which two people in the picture are
    wearing pants?

5. Is anyone wearing eyeglasses?

6. Is Eric wearing a tie? A striped shirt?
    A short jacket?